Crawfish Hunt

Felice Arena and Phil Kettle

illustrated by
Mitch Vane

First published 2003 by
MACMILLAN EDUCATION AUSTRALIA PTY LTD
627 Chapel Street, South Yarra, Australia 3141

This edition first published in the United States of America
in 2004 by MONDO Publishing.

For information contact:
MONDO Publishing
980 Avenue of the Americas
New York, NY 10018
Visit our web site at http://www.mondopub.com

04 05 06 07 08 09   9 8 7 6 5 4 3 2 1

ISBN 1-59336-358-3 (PB)

Library of Congress Cataloging-in-Publication Data

Arena, Felice, 1968-
   [Yabby hunt]
   Crawfish hunt / Felice Arena and Phil Kettle ; illustrated by Mitch Vane.
   p. cm. -- (Boyz rule!)
   Previously published under the title: Yabby Hunt. South Yarra, Australia:
   Macmillan Education Australia Pty, c2003.
   Summary: Matt and Nick decide to go to the local dam to catch some
   crawfish. Includes related miscellanea as well as questions to test the
   reader's comprehension.
   ISBN: 1-59336-358-3 (pbk. : alk. paper)
   [1. Fishing--Fiction. 2. Crayfish--Fiction.] I. Kettle, Phil, 1955- II. Vane,
   Mitch, ill. III. Title.

PZ7.A6825Cr 2004
[E]--dc22

                                                    2004047054

Project Management by Limelight Press Pty Ltd
Cover and text design by Lore Foye
Illustrations by Mitch Vane

Printed in Hong Kong

Contents

Nick   *Matt*

CHAPTER 1

Hot Day

It's a really hot day. Matt and Nick are sitting in their tree house talking.

Matt "Boy, it's hot. Maybe we should go to the dam for a swim."

Nick "Yeah, it's probably too hot for even the aliens to attack today!"

Matt "Last time I swam in the dam, a crawfish bit me on the toe."

Nick "It must have been really hungry—how could anything want to eat what's been inside your sneakers?"

Matt "My shoes don't smell as bad as yours."

Nick "Yeah, right. Your shoes smell like there's cow poop in them."

Matt "Why don't we go catch some crawfish in the dam?"

Nick "Okay. There's s'posed to be lots there—we could get a bucketful then take a swim."

Matt "First we have to get some bait and a bucket to put them in."

Nick "What can we use for bait?"

Matt "I saw Mom take some meat out of the freezer this morning—we might be able to use some of that."

Nick "Yeah, and we could get some string from my place to use as a line."

Matt "I'll get the vegetable strainer to scoop up the crawfish with, when we drag 'em in."

Nick "And I'll get the bucket."

Matt "Cool, and we should take some food...for us."

Nick "Yeah, catching crawfish always makes you hungry."

Matt "How big do you think the crawfish are in the dam?"

Nick "Well, you know Mr. Jones, who lives down the road?"

Matt "Yeah."

Nick "Ya know how he's got one leg missing?"

Matt "Yeah."

Nick "Well, I heard that he went swimming in the dam and a huge crawfish bit his leg off."

Matt "Yeah, right. I heard that a shark bit it off—he fought the shark but it got most of his leg. They tried to sew what was left back on but it was too mangled."

Nick "Really? So what did he do then?"

Matt "He took his leg to the dam and fed it to the crawfish and that's why they're so big!"

CHAPTER 2

Getting Ready

Nick and Matt walk back to Matt's place. Matt's mom gives them some meat to use as bait and makes some sandwiches for the boys to take.

Matt "When we get to your place, do you think your mom will give us some of those cookies we had last week?"

Nick "If there's any left—I think I might have eaten them all."

The boys collect a bucket and some string from Nick's house. There are some cookies left, so Nick's mom packs them in a lunch box and also gets out a bottle of juice for them to take.

Matt "We've got enough food to last us all day."

Nick "Yeah, and if we run out we can always eat some of the crawfish."

CHAPTER 3

Big Crawfish

It isn't long before the boys are at
the dam. They tie pieces of meat to
the end of the string and test out the
length of their lines in the dam.

Matt "How do you know when
  you've got a crawfish on the line?"

Nick "Haven't you ever caught
  crawfish before?"

Matt "Well, I caught the one that bit
  me on the toe."

Nick "Don't you mean the crawfish caught you? When you got out of the dam, it was still hanging on to your toe."

Matt "Well, at least I got it out of the dam, so that's the same as catching one."

Nick "Okay, let's do it for real. Tie one end of the string around your finger, and when a crawfish grabs the meat on the other end you'll feel it pull."

Matt "Then what do you do?"

Nick "You pull it in really slow while I sneak the catcher...y'know, the strainer...under the crawfish and lift it out of the water."

Matt "Okay. That sounds pretty simple."

Nick and Matt sit on the bank with their lines in the water. It isn't long before Matt thinks he has a crawfish on his line.

Matt "I've got one. I can feel the line moving!"

Nick "Well, start to bring it in real slow. I'll get the catcher."

Matt "It feels huge."

Nick "Maybe it's the one that ate
  Mr. Jones's leg!"

Nick picks up the strainer and gets
ready to scoop up the crawfish as
soon as he can see it.

Matt "I see the crawfish coming."
Nick "Just keep pulling it
in...slowly."

Nick sneaks the catcher under the
crawfish and scoops it up.

Matt "Wow, that's the biggest crawfish I've ever seen—not as big as the one that grabbed my toe that time, but almost."

Nick "Well, it's my turn to catch one now."

Matt "Let's have something to eat first."

Nick "Food is the only thing on your mind...ever!"

Matt "No, it's not. There are lots of things I think about."

CHAPTER 4

What if...?

Nick and Matt sit on the bank and begin to eat the food that their mothers made for them.

Matt "Crawfish look like monsters."

Nick "How bad would they be if they were the same size as people?

Matt "Pretty bad...the world would be run by crawfish."

Nick "Yeah, if a crawfish saw you walking down the street and didn't like you, it could just chop you in half."

Matt "And how bad would it be if you had to shake hands with Mr. Crawfish?"

Nick "That'd be the last time you'd ever see your hand."

Matt "How come crawfish can breathe when they are out of water?"

Nick "Maybe they have air tanks
under their shell so they can stay
underwater for longer."

Matt "Yeah. So I wonder if crawfish
used to live on land."

Nick "Maybe. But then they got sick
of being stepped on, so they headed
for the water and stayed there."

Matt "So where do they get their air tanks from?"

Nick "Dunno, but I bet they don't buy them at a store!"

Matt "I'm going to ask my dad when we get home—he knows about all that sort of stuff."

Nick "Yeah, I'll ask my mom too. She told me that crawfish taste good, so she'd have to know."

CHAPTER 5

Second Thoughts

Nick and Matt finish eating all their food then go back to catching more crawfish. Very soon the bucket is almost full.

Matt "This is way too easy, catching crawfish."

Nick "That's only 'cause we're really good at it."

Matt "So what are we going to do with all these crawfish?"

Nick "Take them home."

Matt "Then where will we put them?"

Nick "We'll cook them and eat them."

Matt "How do you cook crawfish?"

Nick "You just put them in hot water and boil them for a while."

Matt "Won't that hurt them?"

Nick "I guess, but that's how you cook them."

Matt "I think we should put them back in the dam. Then we can catch them again another day."

Matt picks up the bucket and before Nick can stop him he's emptied it into the dam.

Matt "We can just say that there weren't any crawfish in the dam after all."

Nick "It can be our secret."

Matt "You wanna go for a swim?"

Nick "Yeah, but I'm keeping my shoes on."

Matt "Well, I'm putting my shoes on *and* leaving all my clothes on. Those crawfish have got really big claws."

Nick

Matt

BOYZ RULE!
Crawfish Catching Lingo

bait A type of food that crawfish usually like to eat. You put bait on the end of your string to attract the crawfish.

cast To throw out your string into the water for the crawfish to grab on to.

crawfish A water creature with a hard shell outside and no internal bones.

dam A body of water a bit like a pond. Often you find a dam on a farm. Dams are good places to catch crawfish.

scoop What you need to get your crawfish on to the bank. A vegetable strainer works well.

BOYZ RULE!

Crawfish Catching Musts

☞ Make sure you ask your mother before you take any meat from the fridge to use as bait.

☞ A piece of string is the best line to use for catching crawfish.

☞ A vegetable strainer makes a good scoop.

☞ Tell your mom where you are going to catch crawfish.

☞ Take your hat and some sunblock with you.

How to catch a crawfish

- Tie a small piece of meat to the end of a length of string.

- Cast the string out about 2 yards (2 meters).

- When you feel a tug on the string, slowly pull in the line.

- When you can see the crawfish, put the scoop under it and lift it up out of the water.

WARNING!

Make sure you don't put your fingers near the crawfish's claws. They can really grip hard!

Put the crawfish you catch in a bucket of water.

Put any really small crawfish you catch back in the dam.

Crawfish Catching
Instant Info

The life span of a crawfish is usually about two to three years.

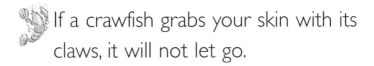
A crawfish can lay up to 800 eggs.

If a crawfish grabs your skin with its claws, it will not let go.

Crawfish claws and legs can grow back if they are broken off.

Crawfish can be kept as pets.

Crawfish will eat almost anything, including goldfish. Sometimes they even eat each other!

Crawfish are also known as crawdads, crayfish, and freshwater lobsters. In Australia they are called yabbies.

Crawfish shed their shell, just like a snake sheds its skin. The new shell takes about two weeks to grow.

There are about 540 different kinds of crawfish; 150 of them can be found in North America.

Think Tank

1 What do Nick and Matt use to catch the crawfish?

2 Can crawfish live out of the water?

3 What does Matt do with the crawfish they've caught?

4 If a crawfish loses a claw, can it grow another one?

5 Where do crawfish live?

6 What would you do if a crawfish bit you on the finger?

7 Would you wear your sneakers to go wading in a stream? Why or why not?

8 If you caught some crawfish, would you throw them back in the water, or take them home to be cooked? Why?

Answers

1 They use pieces of red meat to catch the crawfish.

2 Most crawfish live only in water, but some kinds come out of the water at night.

3 Matt throws the crawfish back in the dam.

4 Yes, a crawfish's claw will grow back.

5 Crawfish mostly live in streams and lakes.

6 Answers will vary.

7 Answers will vary.

8 Answers will vary.

How did you score?

- If you got most of the answers correct, then you will be able to catch a crawfish.

- If you got half of the answers correct, be careful—a crawfish might bite you on the finger!

- If you got less than half of the answers correct, then make sure all you do is look at crawfish in a fish tank!

Felice → ← Phil

Hi guys!

We have lots of fun reading and want you to, too. We both believe that being a good reader is really important and so cool.

Try out our suggestions to help you have fun as you read.

At school, why don't you use "Crawfish Hunt" as a play and you and your friends can be the actors. Set the scene for your play. Find some props and use your imagination to pretend that you are at your favorite pond and just about to start catching crawfish.

So...have you decided who is going to be Matt and who is going to be Nick? Now, with your friends, read and act out our story in front of the class.

We have a lot of fun when we go to schools and read our stories. After we finish, the kids all clap really loudly. When you've finished your play your classmates will do the same. Just remember to look out the window—there might be a talent scout from a television station watching you!

Reading at home is really important and a lot of fun as well.

Take our books home and get someone in your family to read them with you. Maybe they can take on a part in the story.

Remember, reading is a whole lot of fun.

So, as the frog in the local pond would say, Read-it!

And remember, Boyz Rule!

Felice

BOYZ RULE!
When We Were Kids

Phil

Felice "Has a crawfish ever grabbed your finger?"

Phil "Yeah, when I was a kid."

Felice "What did you do?"

Phil "Well, first I screamed. Then I danced around and tried to shake it off."

Felice "And then?"

Phil "I pleaded for it to let go. I even said 'pretty please'."

Felice "And did that work?"

Phil "Nah, so I yelled out the worst words a crawfish could ever hear."

Felice "And what were they?"

Phil "Cooking pot! Cooking pot!"

BOYZ RULE!
What a Laugh!

Q Why does a crawfish never share?

A Because it's shellfish!